TREASURE HUNT

REALITY
SHOW

TREASURE
HUNT

NIKKI SHANNON SMITH

MINNEAPOLIS

Darby Creek
A division of Lerner Publishing Group, Inc.
241 First Avenue North
Minneapolis, MN 55401 USA

For reading levels and more information, look up this title at www.lernerbooks.com.

Cover photographs: Goran Bogicevic/Shutterstock.com (key); Dr. Norbert Lange/Shutterstock.com (maze).

Main body text set in Janson Text LT Std 12/17.5.
Typeface provided by Adobe Systems.

Library of Congress Cataloging-in-Publication Data

Names: Smith, Nikki Shannon, 1971– author.
Title: Treasure Hunt / by Nikki Shannon Smith.
Description: Minneapolis : Darby Creek, [2019] | Summary: Told from separate viewpoints, combative siblings Jazmine, seventeen, and Jason, fifteen, must learn to work together to succeed in a popular television show, Treasure Hunt.
Identifiers: LCCN 2018011860 (print) | LCCN 2018018434 (ebook) | ISBN 9781541541870 (eb pdf) | ISBN 9781541540248 (lb : alk. paper)
Subjects: | CYAC: Reality television programs—Fiction. | Television—Production and direction—Fiction. | Treasure hunt (Game)—Fiction. | Competition (Psychology)—Fiction. | Brothers and sisters—Fiction. | African Americans—Fiction.
Classification: LCC PZ7.S6566 (ebook) | LCC PZ7.S6566 Tre 2019 (print) | DDC [Fic]—dc23

LC record available at https://lccn.loc.gov/2018011860

Manufactured in the United States of America
1-45229-36611-8/9/2018

To "Team Smithereens"

Jazmine

I stared at the pile of textbooks on my desk, then at the list of college application essays I still needed to write. I'd been working non-stop for all of senior year, but I wasn't done yet. College applications were due in two weeks. *There's no way I'm going to get all this done and still have time to study for Friday's chemistry test,* I thought, panicking. *I'll just have to focus on—*

Suddenly the TV turned on, interrupting my thoughts. Jason had flopped down on the couch and started flipping through channels.

"Seriously, Jason? Can't you see I'm doing homework?"

"But *Treasure Hunt* is starting!" Jason whined. "Come watch it with me!"

I rolled my eyes. He was always in my space, pestering me to hang out with him. "Go watch it somewhere else. I've got too much to do."

"But Jaz, we always watch it together!"

"That's because you never leave me alone!" I snapped.

Before Jason could respond, our other brother, Brian, walked in. He sniffled, wiping at his eyes.

"Hey, bud, what's wrong?" Jason asked, jumping up.

Between sniffles, Brian told us that his brand new bike had been stolen. And that Mom and Dad wouldn't buy him another one because it was too expensive. Jason and I just looked at each other, our argument already forgotten. We can't stand it when Brian cries. It's the saddest thing in the world because he's always grinning.

I couldn't figure out what to say. The TV was on so loud that all I could hear was some over-enthusiastic announcer telling viewers to apply for the next season of *Treasure Hunt*. I'd never admit it to Jason, but the show was actually pretty good. Five teams of two competed against one another in a two-day race across America. They had to solve puzzles and finish a physical challenge to get to the $20,000 treasure.

"We should just go on *Treasure Hunt*," I said before I could stop myself. "When we win the money, we could buy you a new bike."

"That's brilliant!" cried Jason.

"No, Jason, I didn't mean it—" I tried to take it back, but one look at Brian stopped me. He was back to his normal self, grinning again. I couldn't disappoint him.

"All right, fine," I said, resigned. "Let's do it." *It's not like we'll be picked, anyway.*

Jason went straight to the computer and printed out all the information. He sat there for what felt like a million years reading through everything.

The first line asked for our team name. That's when the problems really started—we couldn't even agree on a name. Jason's only fifteen, so his name suggestions were dumb. He seriously wanted to write Team Smack Down on the form. I suggested Team Brainiac, but Jason shook his head. We went back and forth with names.

Jason said, "Team Ferrari."

"That's random. Team IQ."

"Team Nike." Jason held out his foot to show me his new Nikes.

I was about to lose it. "That doesn't even make any sense!"

My voice got louder and louder as I listed more ideas, but Jason just kept shaking his head. Finally, I walked over to the table where he was sitting and told him to move. I would just write in something myself.

Jason stood up, but he didn't get out of the way. Even though I'm two years older than him, he's about three inches taller than me. And a lot stronger.

"Move!" I tried to reach the table.

Jason stood in front of me and said, "We need to agree."

I tried to get around him again. Jason planted his feet and crossed his arms.

"This is ridiculous!" I yelled. "Just let me choose the name. Your ideas are horrible."

Just as our dad came into the family room to intervene, Brian said, "How about Team Williams?" He smiled sweetly at us.

Jason just sat back down and wrote it in. It was pitiful that we needed our little brother to solve our arguments, but that's what usually happened.

Jason gets on my last nerve. He's just always there. Every time I turn around he's in my face trying to tell me something. He's always inviting me to do something with him, like watch TV or walk to the store or play a game. But I don't have time for that. I have too much homework. Not to mention college applications.

Anyway, we got the show's application done, recorded the video introducing ourselves, and mailed it in. I forgot all about it after that.

CHAPTER 2

Jason

Brian was really upset when his bike got stolen. It was special to him. He earned it by getting good grades. The bike was the exact model he wanted, and it cost my parents a *lot* of money.

Bri deserved a new bike. I liked Jaz's idea to go on *Treasure Hunt* and use the prize money to buy him a new one. That's why I said I'd go too.

I read all the directions on the application twice. I didn't skip anything. Jaz may have been joking, but I wanted them to pick us. I didn't like the name Team Williams, and I didn't like Jaz's weird attitude, but I'd do anything for my little brother. If I did a good job on the paperwork, maybe we'd actually get picked.

It took twenty-six days for the show to get back to us. I was the one who picked up the phone when they called. Jaz was doing homework. My mom was outside playing catch with Brian. My dad was cooking dinner. He looked at me like I was losing my mind when I started hollering.

When Brian found out we were going on the show, all you could see were his teeth. When he threw his arms around my waist and hugged me so tight it hurt, I knew we had to win.

Jazmine

When Jason started screaming, I raced downstairs to see what was going on. At first I couldn't understand what he was talking about because he was talking really fast. My dad's pasta was boiling over, and my mom had a concerned expression on her face.

Brian ran up to me and gave me a big hug. "Thank you, thank you, thank you!"

His little face hadn't been that happy since the day he got his bike. That's when I figured out what was going on—we'd been picked for *Treasure Hunt*.

I started to panic as a million thoughts

ran through my mind at once. First of all, we weren't *supposed* to get picked. Second of all, I didn't want to miss school. I also didn't want to deal with Jason for two days without my parents. *And I really don't want to be on TV.*

Brian was dancing and singing the Mr. Beefy Burger jingle from his favorite commercial. He spun and yelled, "Fannnnn-taste-ic!" I really didn't want to do the show, but after seeing him so happy it made me realize what I had to do. I would go on the show, and I would be the best. I'd solve all their riddles, complete their challenges, and find the treasure. *And I'll buy you that bike, Brian,* I thought.

Then another thought came to me: if I won this, I was going to be rich. That bike wasn't $20,000. I'd have a lot of money left. I could pay out of state college fees with that. I wouldn't be stuck close to home after all!

My last thought was about my hair. I needed to get it braided. I didn't want to end up with my hair all over my head by the second day of the show. That was not a good look.

Jason

After my parents, Jaz, and I signed the *Treasure Hunt* contract, the show's producers sent us an information packet. It didn't come until the day before the show started filming. Jaz said she read it, but I know she just skimmed it before she went back to her homework. Nobody can read that fast—not even Jaz.

But I read the whole thing. If we were going to win, one of us needed to be ready. The packet said we couldn't bring anything except socks and underwear. No cell phones. No tablets. No snacks. No money. They would give us a backpack with supplies, and that was all we could have. We couldn't even call our family. There would be a chaperone for every team, but we wouldn't know who they were or where they were. They would only step in if there was a problem.

I couldn't wait for this. Maybe Jaz would actually talk to me, since she wouldn't be busy worrying about homework or college.

The night before we started the show, my mom came into my room and sat on my bed. She gave me a serious look and said, "I need you to keep the peace, Jason." I knew exactly what she was talking about too. I promised her I would try, but keeping the peace with Jaz wasn't easy. I only slept about two hours that night.

A limo picked up the whole family early the next morning. Brian looked like one of the kids in the Mr. Beefy Burger commercial— his eyes bulged and he had a huge smile on his face. My parents stared out the window, and Jaz read a book. I didn't know how she could focus on homework at a time like this—I couldn't stop thinking about what

they were going to make us do to find
the treasure.

Four hours later, we got to a town with
a lot of trees. I knew we were still in
California, but this small town didn't look
like the California I knew. A big crowd of
people stood on the sidewalks, waving at us
like we were NBA players or something. A
huge banner read, "Welcome to Lindale,
Treasure Hunters!" The limo stopped in front
of an old brick building that said Chamber of
Commerce over the door. Other limos were
already there, and another one was pulling up.

A woman wearing a suit opened the limo
door. "Hello, Team Williams!" she said,
smiling. "My name is Sonia, and I'm here
to get you started. Jason and Jazmine,
please follow me!" We followed her down a
long hallway.

After we passed door after door, Sonia said,
"This is your prep room, Jason." She opened
the door and told me to go in and change.

Jaz looked nervous, so I held up my hand
for a high five. "This is gonna be fun," I

promised her. She gave me a small smile and a weak pat on my palm. Sonia shut the door behind them.

A few seconds later, I heard Sonia say, "And this is your room, Jazmine." Then a door slammed closed. *That was probably Jazmine*, I thought, shaking my head.

The room I was in was somebody's office. I wondered if they knew some dude was changing clothes in it. There was a red warm up suit laid out on the desk. I put it on and sat down in the big office chair, wondering where *Treasure Hunt* would take us.

Jazmine

After I was dressed, Sonia came back to get me, and Jason was already with her. I froze when I saw we were wearing identical outfits. We were going to look like complete idiots. Everyone at school was going to see us like this.

Jason didn't seem to mind. He chatted away with Sonia as we walked. I gritted my teeth, reminding myself to focus on the money to make it through this ordeal.

Sonia gathered the rest of the teams, and we stood in line until the doors swung open. I was happy to see they were wearing matching clothes too. My body was shivering with nerves—it was the first time in my life I was glad to be at the end of a line. The moment we stepped outside, my thoughts were drowned out by noise. We were surrounded by crowds of screaming people. There were at least fifteen cameras looking at us from every angle—there was even one behind us. I tried to find my parents, but there were too many people. I practically jumped out of my skin when a loud voice blasted out of the speakers: "Here they are, folks! Let's hear it for our treasure hunterrrrrrrrs!"

We followed an escort through the crowd. My heart was pounding and my legs felt like I had twenty-pound weights around my ankles, but Jason acted like he was famous. He clapped and fake jogged like basketball players do when they come out onto the court.

That's when I spotted Brian. He jumped up and down, clapping. When our eyes met, he gave me a thumbs-up. I grinned, elbowed Jason, and pointed to Brian. We gave him a thumbs-up at the same time, which I know looked dorky, but I didn't care. One of the

cameras swung around and aimed at Brian.
He busted some dance moves and made faces.
I couldn't help but laugh. I definitely needed
something to distract me from my nerves.

Finally the crowd parted as we reached
an open clearing. There were ropes blocking
it off so people would stay out. We were in
the middle of a big city park that had a whole
bunch of different activities—sports fields,
a playground, a skateboard area, and a little
amusement park. There was a big stage with
five small platforms on it.

When all five teams reached their
platforms, we were introduced to the
crowd and the cameras. You could tell who
everybody's families were because they
whooped for their own kids. Jason nodded and
smiled at everyone, including our competitors,
but I took the opportunity to size up the
other teams.

First, there was Team Double Trouble.
They were identical twin girls with matching
afro puffs. They looked a little stuck up. Both
of them gazed out at the crowd like they'd

already won. I picked out their parents and almost laughed out loud. They were dressed alike too—they both had on Harvard hoodies. *We'll see if the Harvard Twins can beat Team Williams*, I thought.

The next team was Team Touchdown, two guys who were obviously varsity football players. It seemed like their entire team had come to give them a big send off. I wasn't too worried about this team either—they looked like they had more muscles than brains. But one of them was pretty cute. When he caught me looking at him, I quickly looked the other way.

Team Heartbeat's two members were apparently from the same marching band. They were the only other boy/girl team. The girl looked nervous—the boy just looked bored.

The last team was Team Red Ponytail, whatever that meant. They had matching red bows in their ponytails and matching scowls on their faces.

Out of all the contestants on *Treasure Hunt*, I was the smallest. But I was always the smallest. I hoped the other teams were underestimating me. Then I could take them by surprise when I kicked their butts. And I *would* kick their butts.

CHAPTER

6

Jason

To me, it looked like the show selected all
different kinds of kids so you couldn't guess
who would win. But none of the teams seemed
better than the others. Some kids looked
strong. Some looked smart. The girls with the
ribbons in their hair looked mean. Some kids,
like me and Jaz, seemed normal. All I knew was
we promised Brian we'd buy him a new bike,
so we had to win. I had an idea for the rest of
that money too. I wanted to buy a new home
theater for our family room—a big flat screen
TV, surround sound, and recliners with cup
holders. I already researched it, and we'd have

enough prize money to buy it all. So I had two reasons to win.

The assistants brought each team a backpack that matched the color of their tracksuits. Another man stood in front of us with a fake gun pointed at the sky. When that gun cracked, it would be game on. We watched *Treasure Hunt* all the time, so I knew what to expect. And I had a strategy.

As soon as the gun went off, the other teams took off running in different directions. Jaz tried to run, but I grabbed her arm. "Hang on," I whispered.

"We're wasting time!" she snapped, trying to yank her arm away.

I bent down and opened the backpack. "Everyone always takes off when they hear the gun, but they don't know where they're going. Let's see what's in the backpack first."

Jaz was furious. "You can't be serious. You want to rummage through a bag of stuff? Right now?"

I pulled out an envelope that said *Treasure Hunt: Clue One*. Jaz's eyes widened, and she snatched the envelope from my hands and tore it open to read the clue.

As I hurried to zip up the bag, I heard Brian through the crowd. "Goooo, Team Williams! Gooooooo."

While one of the camera people filmed us, Jaz read the clue out loud:

Hickory, dickory, dock.
We hope you beat the clock.
To find a clue, just work as two.
We're watching like a hawk.
Twinkle, twinkle little star,
The clue is near and not too far.
Up above the world so high,
A wife in a pumpkin in the sky.
Twinkle, twinkle little star,
Smile for the camera, we know where you are.

"I don't get it," I said. I turned around slowly, looking for something that made sense. "There's a big clock on top of that building, though. Maybe it goes with *hickory, dickory, dock?*"

From behind the rope, Brian shrieked, "Hurry up!"

I couldn't focus with all the noise around me. "Read it again," I said.

Jaz grabbed my hand and started running. The moisture from the grass soaked through the toes of my new shoes.

"Where are we going?" I trusted Jaz because she was smart, but if she was wrong, we would waste a lot of time.

She ran through a basketball game, almost knocked down some little kids at the playground, and stopped in front of an amusement park. As soon as she caught her breath she said, "I noticed this when we were in the car. Look."

"Mother Goose's House?" I asked, reading the big banner that stretched over the entrance. Jaz must have been paying more attention on our way to Lindale than I thought. I hadn't seen the amusement park— and I was actually looking.

"The clues are all parts of nursery rhymes!" She dragged me through the gate and stopped at a sign with a map on it. She shoved the paper at me and told me to read it again while she looked at the map.

I checked to see if anyone else was coming. No one was there but the camera guy. I started reading.

Jazmine groaned. "Can you read faster?"

She snatched the clue and read it herself. I felt my face heat up as I realized the camera had caught that. Jaz was making us both look bad. She put her finger on the map and traced a path with it. She tapped her finger on the middle of the map. "Peter's Eaters."

"What?"

Jaz rolled her eyes. "Peter, Peter pumpkin eater, had a wife but couldn't keep her. You know . . . the nursery rhyme? The park's food court is called Peter's Eaters!"

Yeah, I know, I thought, *but I don't know what this has to do with the clue.*

Before I could ask another question, she took off running again. For someone with short legs, she was fast. I followed her over a little bridge, past a gigantic shoe, under a moon with a cow jumping over it, and almost bumped into her when she stopped at a little food court.

Jazmine pointed to the top of the hut where people can order food. "Get up there."

"Huh?"

Jaz growled. "The clue is in the pumpkin on top of the building."

I didn't know how she figured that out, but I didn't question her. Even though Jaz was annoying, I knew she was probably right. I jumped up and grabbed the metal bar that went all the way around the roof. I looked down at her. "Push me up."

"I can't. You're too heavy."

"Get under me. I have an idea."

For once Jaz listened to me. I made her squat down, and I put my feet on her shoulders. While she straightened up, I pulled myself up with my arms. Before I knew it, I was on the roof, crawling toward the pumpkin. There was an open window in it, with a fake lady staring out.

"Go in and get the clue!"

I looked down at her. "I can't fit."

Jaz put her hands on her hips, sighed, and gave me a fake smile that I knew meant *figure it out*. I walked around the pumpkin, but there was no other way in. I stood at the window. It seemed like Peter's girl was laughing at me. I was staring at her scary looking make-up when I noticed some envelopes barely sticking out of her shirt. I snatched one. The envelope said *Treasure Hunt: Clue Two*. I swung down from the roof and handed the paper to Jaz.

Jazmine

If all of the clues came as naturally to me as the first one, the other teams had zero chance of winning.

Right after Jason handed me the second clue we heard yelling somewhere in the park. I grabbed his wrist. "Hide," I said.

As usual, Jason looked confused, so I ran toward the back corner of the park, pulling him behind me. The camera guy followed us, and when I ducked behind a fake pile of hay, he did too.

"Why are we hiding?" asked Jason.

"Because, if the other teams see us, they'll

know where the clue is," I whispered.

Jason nodded.

I opened the envelope. It had a bunch of papers inside. The first was a train schedule. I handed it to Jason. "Start looking through this."

Next, there was a copy of a news article about a place called Hotel Telegraph. Last, there was a bag of tile letters—and there were only seven of them.

"Are there train tickets in there?" I asked Jason, who was still studying the schedule.

"Nope."

"Well, did you find anything in there at all?"

"No," said Jason, looking confused. "It's just a schedule with a map of the train stations."

Okay, Jaz, think. You've got this. I gave myself a pep talk, but I could tell I was starting to panic—this was taking too long.

I dumped out the tile letters. Jason helped me turn them all over. Y. T. E. G. N. O. R. I told Jason to look at the papers again and I started rearranging the letters. T-O-N-E-G-R-Y. T-R-Y-G-O-N-E. G-R-O-N-E-T-Y. Nothing was making sense. G-R-E-N-T-O-Y.

To make matters worse, Jason wasn't doing what I told him to do—instead, he was looking through the brochure about Hotel Telegraph. I snatched the train schedule out of his other hand and looked at it myself.

"What if the letters spell a stop on the train route?"

Jason stared at me.

I handed him the schedule. "Read me the names." That was a mistake. Slow and steady was not going to win this race. I looked over his shoulder and read it myself. "There! Greyton! We need tickets to Greyton."

"Yeah, that makes sense!" Jason said, excited. "Hotel Telegraph is in Greyton too! I bet that means we're supposed to go there to look for more clues."

"Perfect. But how are we supposed to get tickets with no money?" I found the prices on the schedule. A ticket to Greyton was $5.50. "What if we have to sneak in?"

Jason didn't answer me. I looked at him, and he was staring at me like I was an idiot. After a long second, he tossed something up in the air. A twenty-dollar bill landed on the schedule.

"You snuck money? You're going to get us disqualified!"

"Nah. It was in the backpack you didn't want me to waste time looking through." Jason smirked.

"How much?"

"A hundred."

CHAPTER 8

Jason

Jaz didn't say a word. She peeked around
the haystack, and then took off again. The
cameraperson, whose name I learned was
Steve, and I followed her out of the park and
down the street. When she got to the corner,
she stopped.

She panted for a minute. "Where is the
train station?"

"How should I know?" *Why did you take off
running if you didn't know where you were going
in the first place?* I thought, irritated. She was
always in a race with her own self. Jaz stood
in one spot and turned from side to side. She

looked lost. It was a good thing Lindale didn't seem like the kind of place where people messed with you on the street.

"What are you—"

Jaz cut me off. "Shhh." Spit sprayed out of her mouth. "I'm listening for trains."

I left her standing on the corner acting like a human satellite. I walked two buildings down to a coffee shop. A woman came out holding a tray full of cups.

"Excuse me," I said. "Do you know where the train station is?"

She looked up and stared at something behind me, so I turned around. It was Steve. Jaz was still on the corner spinning around.

"Are you one of the contestants on *Treasure Hunt*? You are, aren't you!" She smiled and flipped her hair at the camera. "Will I be on TV?"

"I don't know, but I need to get to the train station. Can you help me?"

"Well . . ."

As she explained the directions, I could tell this lady wanted every second of fame she could get. But I needed her help and didn't want to make her mad, so I had to wait through it.

As I ran back to Jaz, the woman yelled, "Good luck!"

I told Jaz the directions, and she said, "How do you know?"

"I asked somebody."

I was happy to see she looked a little ashamed, like she felt dumb for not thinking of that herself. *Sometimes smart people think too much*, I thought. *Or maybe they just can't imagine needing help.*

We ran all the way to the train station. Even more people recognized us as contestants, and they took pictures and clapped. I realized I would probably like being famous. As long as I wasn't racing against the clock trying to win $20,000 with Jaz telling me what to do.

Jazmine

Jason thought he was so smart for getting us to the train station. He had a smug look on his face while we sat on the platform waiting. I didn't want to admit it, but we'd gotten here thanks to him.

"So," said Jason. "How did you figure out the clue was in the pumpkin?"

"The clue was all nursery rhymes, so I figured it had to be inside Mother Goose's House. I didn't know what the middle meant, but when I saw Peter's Eaters on the map, I knew it went with *a wife in a pumpkin in the sky*. The rest was easy." I smiled at the camera.

Out of the corner of my eye, I saw two guys wearing yellow run onto the platform. It was Team Touchdown. It didn't matter if one of them was cute; I did not want them anywhere near us.

They saw us before we had a chance to hide and had the nerve to come over to where we were. "Hey," said the tallest one, like he thought he was cool.

Jason nodded at them. I gave him a fake smile, and I could tell he got the point. This was not a football game and I was not a fan. Luckily, the train pulled up. I wanted to get as far away from them as I could, but instead I got on the same train car and sat a couple of seats away, facing them. *Keep your friends close and your enemies closer*, I thought.

The ride to Greyton was only about twenty minutes. When we arrived, I took my time getting off the train.

"Why are you going so slow?" Jason asked. He had a lot of nerve. He was the king of slow.

"I don't want them following us."

Greyton was the opposite of Lindale. It was a big city, and people were everywhere. There were no trees, no flowers, and no parks. Steam that smelled like boiled eggs drifted up from a grate in the street. If I hadn't committed to winning *Treasure Hunt* I would probably turn around and take the train right back to where we started.

We stood on the sidewalk trying to figure out what to do next. A woman bumped into me and didn't even apologize. Team Touchdown disappeared into the crowd.

I read the article about Hotel Telegraph on the train, and it wasn't very helpful. It only talked about the upcoming fifty-year anniversary, who built the hotel, and how some famous people I had never heard of had stayed there.

Jason said, "Let's get directions."

"I'm not talking to some random person on the street. That's your department." I didn't like talking to strangers. I stood behind Jason while he asked a man how to get to Hotel Telegraph.

After ten minutes of walking, I saw Team Touchdown ahead of us. They went into a building with green flags hanging above the door. The flags said Hotel Telegraph in fancy white letters.

A wrinkle appeared between Jason's eyebrows. "Maybe we shouldn't have let them get ahead of us."

We needed to keep moving. I ducked into the hotel and pulled Jason behind a fountain in the lobby. The football players stood at the front desk. After a few minutes, they got on an elevator with a cameraperson right behind them.

Once the elevator doors closed, we went to the front desk.

"Excuse me, but what did those guys say?" I asked the receptionist.

He gave me a funny look. "Something about a clue. I don't have no idea what they were talking about."

"Well, what did you tell them?" I could barely keep the exasperation out of my voice. This guy was slowing us down.

The man leaned forward. "I told them I didn't know what they were talking about."

I leaned forward too, but before I could say anything else, Jason thanked the man and led me away.

Jason

I knew that if I didn't step in soon, Jazmine was going to get us cussed out. "We're wasting our time with him," I said. That, at least, she understood.

I got her away from the desk, and she stood in the middle of the lobby with her hands on her hips. "Well, I say we at least check out the lobby, but we better hurry up before the other teams get here."

The hotel was really old fashioned and smelled like our grandma. *This isn't going to work*, I thought as I looked at all the ornate furniture. *The show wouldn't have us waste our time searching this whole hotel.* But Jazz was on a mission, so I sighed and got started.

We dug through the dirt in all the potted plants but didn't find anything. Jaz peeked behind the red velvet curtains, and I checked behind the gold-framed paintings on the wall. A woman sitting in a chair that looked like a throne closed her book and watched us. We didn't find a single clue.

"Now what?" I asked.

Jaz pointed. "The sofa cushions. I'll take this couch, you take that one."

I felt like the robbers in movies who turned the house upside down looking for stuff. I guess the guy from the front desk thought we looked suspicious because he walked up to me and cleared his throat. "What do you think you're doing?"

I put the cushion down and gave it a little pat. "Nothing," I said.

Jaz rushed over. "We're on a reality show called *Treasure Hunt*. We're looking for clues to where the treasure is."

The man looked at Steve. "Is this one of

those shows where you try to irritate people to see what they'll do?"

Steve said, "No, sir."

The man frowned. "I don't know what's wrong with everyone today, but there are no clues here. If you don't leave right now, I'm calling the police."

Jaz rolled her eyes. "Fine."

When we got back outside, she just stood there looking confused. Finally she said, "Well, there has to be something about this place."

Jaz was right. Maybe the employees didn't know about it. Or maybe it was on the outside somewhere. Or maybe we missed something when we read the article.

"Jaz, maybe we should read through that article again."

Suddenly her eyes got big. "We need to hide," she said, panicking.

But there was nowhere to hide. Plus, we were wearing matching red clothes, so it wasn't like we could blend in. Not to mention Steve stood there like a big advertisement. I didn't see any reason to hide anyway.

"Team Double Trouble is coming!" Jaz's voice was about three times higher than normal. "Everyone is gaining on us."

Jaz was seriously about to lose it. I told her to take the article out and act confused. I snatched the article out of her hand and frowned at it. I held it close to my face and moved my lips. I could see Team Double Trouble out of the corner of my eye.

They laughed at me, and one said, "Read much?"

"Shut up," said Jaz. Steve pointed his camera in Jaz's face. I tried to read her face to see if she was just acting for the camera, but she actually seemed really angry at the twins.

They laughed again and walked into the hotel.

I couldn't believe she stood up for me. "Thanks," I said.

Jaz just shrugged like it was no big deal. "Whatever."

Even though I was trying to make them think we were stuck, they hit a nerve. I gave the paper back to Jaz, and she read it to me. She wasn't a jerk about it either. When she finished I shook my head. There were no clues.

Jaz is gonna get antsy just standing still like this, I thought. *We have to do something.* I glanced around and saw a woman handing out papers to anyone walking by who would take one. Not sure what else to do, I took a step toward her, but Jaz stopped me. "I don't think you should bother anyone."

I went anyway. "Hi, I was wondering—"

"Let me guess!" she said, beaming. "You were wondering what my newsletter says."

"Well, not really. But—"

"It's the people's newsletter. I put everything that happens in this area in it."

Before I could think of what to say, she handed me one of her carefully folded newsletters and winked.

Jazmine

I crossed my arms, tapped my foot, and waited for Jason to finish talking to the lady. *He always does this*, I thought. *He just loves being a social butterfly.* After what felt like forever, Jason walked back toward me, glancing down at the newsletter.

"Don't even think about reading that thing," I said.

He was about to argue, so I made him put the newsletter in the backpack. I led him and Steve around the side of the hotel.

The alley smelled like pee, and the two big dumpsters were so full the lids wouldn't close. A cat jumped from a ledge onto the ground in front of us and hissed. Jason wrinkled his nose in disgust. "I don't think the *Treasure Hunt* people would send us down a dirty alley."

"Yeah, let's turn around," I said.

"Maybe they have a backyard or a courtyard." Jason snuck around the cat and past the dumpsters with Steve trailing behind him. "Stay there," he called over his shoulder.

I was not about to stay by myself, so I followed him around the corner of the building. The back of the hotel was whatever the opposite of a backyard was. It wasn't any bigger than the alley, and there was garbage piled up against the building. We saw a shadow move and took off running.

This whole thing was turning into one big, stupid wild goose chase, and Jason wasn't doing anything to help. He took the newsletter out of the backpack.

"Seriously?" I said.

"She sees everything. Maybe one of her articles has a clue." Jason frowned, giving the newsletter a shake. "Wait a second. It feels like there's something in here."

"Then maybe you shouldn't open it. There's no telling what's in there."

He unfolded the newsletter and took out two small, rectangular papers. They were plane tickets. I leaned in closer, reading over his shoulder. We'd been booked on a flight to Texas—today.

"Oh, man," Jason groaned, his brown face turning gray.

"What?"

He shook his head. "I don't want to go."

"We don't have a choice, Jason. Our flight leaves in, like, three hours. We have to go now!" He stared down at the tickets. "What's the matter with you?"

Jason's cheeks turned pink. "I don't want to fly."

I'd wanted to fly my whole life. We always drove when we went on vacations because my dad said it was the best way to see the world. I couldn't believe Jason didn't want to go.

"You can't be serious," I said.

Jason didn't answer me. He turned his back to the camera and took a bunch of deep breaths. *What is going on with him?* I wondered. *Is he really that afraid to fly?*

We'd never taken a taxi before either, but we needed to get to the airport—whether Jason liked it or not. I'd seen people wave down taxis in movies too many times to count, so I figured it couldn't be that hard. As one came around the corner, I flagged it down and it pulled right over. It was just as easy as the movies made it look.

"How far is it to the airport?" I asked.

"About fifteen minutes," the driver said.

"How much will you charge to take us there?"

"Depends on the time. Probably about forty dollars."

That sounded high to me. I looked at Jason, but he was no help because he was still freaking out about flying. If we spent half of our money on the first day, we could run out and be stuck somewhere and lose. But we needed to get there fast, and we didn't really have another option.

We got in the cab, and the driver stepped on the gas so hard our heads snapped back. Steve grunted. Jason put his head in his hands. This was going to be a long trip.

Jason

Jaz stared at me for the first five minutes of the cab ride. I could feel her eyes on my neck while I stared out the window. My hands started to sweat, and I nervously wiped them on my tracksuit pants. Jaz's stares didn't help, either. *Relax, Jason*, I tried to tell myself. *People fly all the time. It'll be fine.*

Finally, Jaz broke the silence. "Is there any food in the backpack?"

I handed her the bag. She must have been starving because she passed over everything else in the bag until she came across some packs of almonds and dried fruit.

"Want some?" She tried to hand me some almonds.

My stomach clenched with nerves. I wished she'd just leave me alone for a while. "No," I said quickly.

She laughed. "You're really scared. Wow."

"Shut up!" I said. I wished Brian was old enough to be on *Treasure Hunt*. Then it might have actually been fun.

For the rest of the ride my stomach was in my throat, and the only sounds were Jaz crunching and the cab driver's music.

When we got to the airport, Jaz paid the driver, and I stood on the curb like I weighed eight hundred pounds. Jaz's eyes raced all over the place reading signs.

"We don't have bags, so we can skip that part," she said. "Okay. There's security." If I wasn't feeling so nervous, I would have been impressed. Jaz somehow knew what to do even though we've never been to an airport. She led me to a long line of people. When we got to the front of the line, a security guard asked us for our boarding passes. Jaz handed him the tickets. Next he asked for our IDs.

"We don't have ID," said Jaz.

"Birth certificate?"

"No."

"No ID, no entry," he said.

Jaz balled up her fists. "We don't have a choice. We're on *Treasure Hunt*. We need to win the money. I'm trying to have enough money for out of state college."

As soon as she said that, I got so mad that I forgot about being scared. *What did she say?! She's got to be kidding!* I thought. *I know she didn't just claim all the money for herself.* Jaz wouldn't have gotten this far without me. She was lucky I couldn't speak because I'd never wanted to tell somebody off this badly in my entire life.

"And we promised my brother a new bike." Jaz was talking twice as fast as normal, completely ignoring the anger on my face.

The man just rolled his eyes. "Next!"

A second security guard stood next to us like she thought something was about to go down. Maybe that was a good idea, since I practically saw smoke coming out of Jazmine's nostrils.

She looked at me. "Do *something*."

But I wasn't about to do one single thing for her. She certainly didn't think about me when she made plans for *our* money. When I didn't answer, she ripped the backpack off my shoulders. "Maybe the *Treasure Hunt* people put something in here."

The backup guard said, "Miss, you'll have to move out of the way."

"Just give me a minute."

"Miss, if you don't move, I will be forced to move you."

Jaz looked at me and then at Steve. She rolled her eyes at the security guard. "Fine."

Jaz marched over to a chair with me trailing about ten feet behind her. She unzipped the backpack and turned it upside down. A bunch of papers, packets of almonds, two bottles of water, and a first aid kit scattered on the floor. *If she would have taken the time to look through the backpack at the beginning like*

I did, she wouldn't need to do this, I thought with a sigh of irritation.

"A-ha!" Jaz cried a few seconds later. She held two papers in the air and flicked her wrists so I could see. "Birth certificates." She scooped everything off the floor and crammed it back into the backpack. Then she marched to the front of the line like she had already won *Treasure Hunt*.

The security guard barely glanced at her. "I'm sorry, miss. You'll have to go to the end of the line."

Jaz got a scary look on her face. "What do you mean, the end of the line?"

The second guard took a step forward, so I grabbed Jaz and dragged her to the back of the line. When we got to the front again, we made it past the checkpoint with no problem and none of the other teams in sight.

At least one good thing came from Jaz's little tantrum: it distracted me from my fear of flying.

CHAPTER 13

Jazmine

After getting past the guards, we had to wait in another line at the security checkpoint. When we finally made it through, I checked the tickets, found our gate, and saw we had about an hour to wait. I couldn't believe how long the security process had taken, and I wasn't looking forward to waiting around even more.

But on the way to the gate, I got happy again. There were restaurants *everywhere*. You could get popcorn, sandwiches, pizza, soda, candy—they had everything. You could go shopping and buy new clothes and a suitcase if you wanted. I headed straight to the pizza place, even though I noticed a bookstore at the last minute. I couldn't really spend money on a book right now anyway.

"What do you want?" I asked Jason.

He just shook his head. Normally I'd insist that he eat something, but he looked like he was going to be sick and I didn't want him throwing up on the plane. I ordered pizza and a soda, and we sat down at a table. As soon as my food came, a little girl bounced over to us. She looked like she was about four. Her hair used to be in two ponytails, but one side was missing a hair tie.

"Hi," she said.

I took a big bite. "Hi."

"I have a present for you." She smiled.

"You do?"

She nodded.

"What is it?"

The little girl handed me a crumpled sticker and a penny, and I thanked her again. She stared at me while I ate, which made me uncomfortable. I noticed Steve filming us, so

I gave the girl a small smile and hoped she'd go away.

Then she handed Jason something that looked like the homemade birthday cards I used to make. He opened it and looked up at me in surprise. "When you get to Texas, report to gate B12," he read aloud.

Jason

Jaz was a different person after she ate. She stood by the window and watched planes take off. It was already getting dark outside. I sat across the room and watched the people. I distracted myself by guessing why they were leaving town. Then they announced our flight was boarding.

Jaz didn't say anything when we got on the plane. I sat in the middle, and she sat next to the aisle. Steve sat a couple seats away in the row across from us.

"No other teams are on this flight," Jaz said as she looked through the rows of seats.

"I think we're back in the lead."

The flight attendants started talking about what to do in an emergency, and Jaz closed her eyes. Now that I was actually on the plane, I started feeling better. I looked through the stack of magazines sitting in a pouch on the seat in front of me as we waited for takeoff.

Soon, a flight attendant stood at the front of the plane and went through safety instructions. When she started talking about landing in water, I could feel my palms getting sweaty. *Calm down, Jason*, I thought to myself. *It will be fine. Just relax—*

I heard Jazmine gasp for breath beside me. I glanced over and saw that her eyes were shut tight and tears ran down her cheeks.

"Jaz?"

She didn't answer.

"Jaz, are you okay? Do you want me to ask Steve to call the chaperone?"

Jaz quickly shook her head, but her body was trembling and I could see beads of sweat forming on her forehead.

"Jaz, are you sick?" As fast as she ate that pizza, it wouldn't surprise me.

Jaz whispered, "My whole face is tingling." She opened her eyes and they were full of fear.

I bet she's having a panic attack, I thought. I'd never seen Jaz like this, and it made me nervous. But I didn't want her to see that I was worried. I did the only thing I could think of and took Jaz's hand. "You need to breathe. In, two, three, four. Out, two, three, four. Close your eyes."

Jaz closed her eyes again and breathed with my counting. Soon her breathing got steadier, and her body started to relax. But I kept counting—it was helping me too. *It's a good thing Steve can't use his camera on the plane*, I thought, relieved.

After what felt like an hour, the plane started to roll backward, and the sound of the engine changed. Then the plane moved forward. It was slower than a car.

Jaz's eyes shot open. "Are we moving?"

I nodded and kept counting. She wiped her face with her sleeve.

"You can stop counting now. I think I'm okay." The plane sped up and Jaz smiled. She giggled as we lifted off the runway. I opened the little shade on the window and we watched the lights on the ground get farther and farther away.

"Thanks, Jason," she said quietly after a few minutes. "I thought you were the one that was afraid of flying, not me."

CHAPTER 15

Jazmine

I couldn't believe I had a panic attack—I didn't even know I was afraid to fly. I waited until the seatbelt light went off, and then I went to the bathroom. My stomach was in knots. By the time I got back to my seat, there was a snack on my tray.

Jason said, "I got you some Ginger Ale."

"Thanks."

"You okay?" he asked.

"Yeah. You?"

"I like it. Think about all the science behind the engine, the wings . . . everything. It's a miracle something this big and heavy can fly. Also, the snacks were free." He popped a cookie into his mouth. He was obviously over his fear of flying. I wasn't so sure about myself.

Jason pulled out some papers from the backpack. "We should read these."

"What are they?"

"Bios. There's a paragraph about every team, and their pictures are at the top."

He handed me two. The top one was about Team Touchdown. I took a minute to look at the cute guy, then I read about how the two had been best friends since kindergarten. The other paper was about Team Double Trouble. Their parents were both Harvard professors. The mom was from Brazil, and the twins were bilingual. *We'll have to watch out for them*, I thought.

When Jason finished reading he said, "I'm pretty sure the girl on Team Heartbeat has a crush on the boy. It was her idea to audition, and apparently the whole *heartbeat* thing was her idea too."

"What's the deal with Team Red Ponytail?" I asked.

"They compete in horse shows. It says if horses have a red ribbon on their tail, it's a warning to other riders that they might kick."

I rolled my eyes. "So, they're saying they're going to kick the competition's butts. Whatever. What about our bio?"

Jason pulled ours out of the stack, and we looked at it together. They used our school pictures. The bio said we were described by our mother as "unlikely teammates who joined forces to do something nice for their little brother." We laughed about the phrase "unlikely teammates."

We spent the rest of the flight joking about the other teams and discussing what advantages we might have over them. For the first time since I could remember, we were actually getting along. Before I knew it, the plane was lowering to land.

We got off the plane and followed the signs to gate B12. I was relieved to see we were the first team there, but the crew of *Treasure Hunt* people in black jackets who waited for us made me nervous.

CHAPTER 16

Jason

Gate B12 was in a different section of the airport that looked like it was closed. There were no people around. When we finally got to the gate, one of the guys in a black jacket handed me a note.

Steve said, "Read it out loud."

I wasn't about to do that on camera again, so I passed the note to Jaz. She cleared her throat and read, "We hope you're not tired. We hope you are strong. The tire is heavy. The runway is long."

The *Treasure Hunt* team walked toward the tunnel that led to a plane, and we followed them. Instead of getting on a plane, they went through a side door and down a set of stairs. We ended up outside in the dark. When we reached the runway at the bottom of the stairs, everyone had to put on headphones. I figured it was because the planes were so loud. The runways looked cool at night. Rows of lights marked the sides, so it looked like a huge highway. We passed four gigantic planes, crossed one of the lanes, and stopped in an area of the runway that was empty. I noticed five tires lying flat in a line, which meant we were the first team there. *If we can do this task and stay ahead, we might actually have a chance to win this thing*, I thought, getting excited.

A voice came through the headphones, and I jumped. "You will now complete the physical challenge of the *Treasure Hunt* competition. You must get your tire from this end of the runway to the other end."

That sounded easy enough. Even though the runway was as long as two football fields and the tires looked like they were from a big rig or a tractor, all we had to do was roll it.

The voice continued. "Keep your tire from touching the ground. If you drop it, you must return to the start line and try again. Good luck—this tire weighs one hundred and fifty pounds."

I weighed more than that, and I could easily imagine two people carrying me to the other end. I knew we could do it. I noticed Jaz saying something to me, but I couldn't hear it. Another person in a black jacket pulled a little mic down from Jaz's headphones and then did the same to mine. *Are they recording all of our conversations?* I wondered.

Jaz said, "Those tires look heavy."

"It's not that bad. There are two of us."

"I think we should just grab it and go as fast as possible, before we get tired."

I wasn't sure that would work. *There has to be a trick to it*, I thought. *They wouldn't give us a challenge where all we have to do is pick it up and walk. That seems too easy.* "Let's test it out," I said.

We stood on either side of the tire, faced each other, and picked it up. The tire was heavy, but it wasn't impossible to lift. The problem was the distance. If our hands got sweaty or sore, we'd drop it.

"Stop thinking," said Jaz. "Let's go."

She started walking, and unless I wanted to start out by dropping the tire, there was nothing I could do but follow her. As soon as we started, a big digital clock at the other end flashed 45:00. It was so dark outside that I hadn't even noticed it before. The clock started counting backward.

"What's that clock for?" I asked through the mic.

"The clock shows the time remaining before the flight to your next destination departs. If you miss it, you will not be disqualified, but you will have to wait for the next flight."

"How long is that?" I asked.

"Two hours."

The tire was lopsided because Jaz was so much shorter than I was. I lowered my side, so she wouldn't get extra weight. We sidestepped toward the finish line. Steve sidestepped next to us, and a woman with a camera on wheels followed. We weren't even halfway there when Jaz started panting into the microphone.

"Do you want me to walk backward?" I asked.

She nodded. We turned so Jaz could walk forward. She sped up right away. "This is way better."

"Not for me. I can't go backward that fast. Slow down."

Jaz blew out a puff of air. "We've already used fifteen minutes. We can't slow down."

I looked at the start line. "No one else is even here yet."

It was like I hadn't said anything at all. Jaz kept pushing me backward, and I struggled to keep the pace. "You're gonna make us drop it!" I yelled.

Jaz's face was sweaty and all twisted up. She walked even faster and I tripped. "You're a jerk. This is why you don't have any friends," I said. "You don't know how to get along with other people." I didn't care if the camera was rolling—it was true, and I was sick of her bossing me around.

"I have friends!" Jaz protested.

"No, you don't. Everyone knows it."

Jaz completely lost it. She screamed at me. "This tire is too heavy and you're too slow and you get on my last nerve!"

"I'm the one who got us to the train station. I'm the one who got the plane tickets from that lady. If we lose, it'll be *your* fault, not mine!"

The tire slipped a little. I stopped walking and leaned into the tire so she'd have to stop. There was no way we were getting to the other end like this. And I was *not* going to let Jaz tell me what to do anymore.

"Do you want to win or not?" I asked.

Jaz didn't answer, but I could tell she was concentrating on calming down. Of course she wanted to win. It wasn't just because she wanted the money for college either. Jazmine always had to win. She always had to be right.

"What if we both walk forward," she said after a few seconds. "Even though we'd be one handed, it would be easier to walk, and we might even be able to jog."

I shook my head. "It's too heavy to do it with one hand."

Jaz held the tire with one hand. She tucked her fingers into the rim so she'd have a good grip. "See? It's easier."

I still wasn't convinced, but decided it was worth a try if it shut her up. After six or seven steps, her muscles started to shake. I felt the tire going down, and I tried to catch it, but I couldn't. Her end hit the ground.

CHAPTER 17

Jazmine

"Seriously, Jason?" I yelled.

He glared at me. "How is this *my* fault? You're the one who dropped it. Always trying to hurry. If you would have slowed your roll, the tire wouldn't have fallen."

"You should have been ready to catch it," I said, fuming. "You know you're stronger than me."

Jason didn't say anything. He just stood the tire up and rolled it back to the start line. By the time we got there, Team Touchdown was picking up their tire. If they were as strong as they looked, they would definitely make the next flight. Less than half the time was left on the clock, so Jason and I would have to run to get to the other side of the runway to make the flight.

Team Touchdown took off down the runway the same way Jason and I did the first time—sidestepping their way there. But they were going fast, and they made it look like their tire weighed twenty pounds.

Jason's slow voice came through the headphones. "Okay, let's try putting it on our shoulders. If we do that, we can both walk forward. Then if you get tired, we can turn our bodies around and switch shoulders."

It actually wasn't a bad idea, but I wasn't about to tell him that. "Fine," I grumbled.

I struggled getting the tire on my shoulder, but I managed to get it. We fast-walked down the runway, with Jason bending down some to take extra weight off of me. Team Touchdown was already at the halfway mark, but there were only twelve minutes until takeoff. There was no way they were going to finish the race, find the gate, and get on the plane in time.

That meant we weren't going to make it either.

The tire dug into my shoulder. "I need to switch sides," I said.

We had to stop walking to adjust the tire, and while I was turning around, I saw Team Heartbeat had also made it onto the runway. They were gaining on us by copying our strategy. *Whatever. None of us are going to make the stupid flight*, I thought.

I watched Team Touchdown cross the finish line, drop the tire, and do a dance that ended with them bumping chests. There were five minutes on the clock. One of the *Treasure Hunt* people handed them something, and they ran up the stairs back into the airport. I tried not to let it distract me. *They're celebrating and running for nothing, they'll never make it.* Everyone else's failure was all I had to hold onto.

The clock had been flashing 00:00 for at least ten minutes by the time we finished. What made it worse was that Team Heartbeat crossed right before us.

The girl smiled at me. "That was crazy, huh?"

"That's one word for it," I said.

Jason

By the time we crossed the finish line with our tire, Jaz looked like she was about to cry. She didn't say a word as the *Treasure Hunt* crew member handed us an envelope with our team name on it and led us back into the airport. I took the envelope and noticed she was cradling her left hand.

"Let me see your hand," I said.

She held it out and I saw that she had cut it on the tire, all the way across three of her fingers. Steve did a close up of her hand. It didn't need stitches or anything, but I walked her to the bathroom and waited while she washed it off. When she finished, I took out the first aid kit that was in our backpack. I wrapped each finger in a bandage.

"Thanks," she said.

I put my arm around her. She was a pain in the butt, but she was still my sister.

"Umm . . . You stink." Jaz took my arm off of her shoulder and laughed.

I shrugged, smirking. "Maybe because I did all the work."

She rolled her eyes and shoved me, but Steve interrupted us. "Jazmine, Jason, tell us what you thought of the tire challenge."

The show always had these little interviews with the teams after certain parts of the hunt. I knew this was going to be on TV. I said, "It was pretty hard. The tire was heavy, and it kept slipping. At least we made it."

"Jazmine, do you have anything to add?" Steve aimed the camera at her.

All she said was, "It was interesting." She turned away from Steve and pulled something out of the envelope. Suddenly her face broke into a grin, and she handed it to me.

I read the ticket. "Seriously? We're going to *New York City*?"

Jaz nodded in excitement, and it was like the Tire Challenge never happened. We had always wanted to go to New York City.

Jaz elbowed me. "Look! Team Touchdown missed the plane too!"

Team Touchdown was sitting in the corner looking like the world's biggest, poutiest babies. I chuckled.

When they announced it was time to board, four teams were at the gate: us, Team Touchdown, Team Heartbeat, and Team Double Trouble. Team Red Ponytail was nowhere in sight. The best part was, now that no one was ahead of us, Jaz relaxed—sort of. We spent the whole flight naming famous people and landmarks in New York.

CHAPTER 19

Jazmine

The flight to New York went a lot better than the one to Texas. And even though we lost our lead, we weren't behind anyone. I was also relieved that we finally had some time to rest. *Treasure Hunt* was a lot of work. No wonder people had bad attitudes by the end of the show. Half the time they wound up hating the other person on their team. They always talked crap about each other in the solo interviews at the very end.

Jason, of course, had us sitting with the other teams on the plane. They were all talking and laughing about the challenges so far like they weren't competing against one another. But I wasn't here to make friends. I was here to win.

My parents said I couldn't go to an out-of-state college because of the higher tuition and the extra fees, but I wanted a major change of scenery. If I won this money, they would have to let me go. I had certainly put in the work to get into those schools.

In the middle of me eavesdropping on all the chattering, we heard a buzzing noise. The girl from Team Heartbeat figured out it was coming from her backpack. Then one by one, we all realized our backpacks were buzzing.

There was a tiny side pocket we hadn't noticed. Inside was a black box. It looked like a cross between a tiny walkie-talkie with no antenna and an old fashioned cell phone.

"What is this?" asked the cute boy from Team Touchdown, looking confused.

Steve cracked up. "A pager."

He frowned. "What's that?"

"It's the grandfather of the smart phone. People used them to get in touch with someone. They typed in their phone number, the pager received it, and the person called them," said Steve.

"So you can't talk on them?" asked one of the twins.

Steve shook his head. I looked at the pager. Instead of a phone number, there was a message: "Team Red Ponytail Disqualified: Altercation."

"Altercation?" asked Jason.

I laughed. "It means they got into some kind of fight. Maybe they kicked somebody."

Now we had a twenty-five percent chance of winning. But since we had been ahead most of the time, I figured it was more like a fifty-fifty chance. I decided it was a good idea to get to know what made everyone tick before we got off the plane, so I chatted with them too—just in case.

CHAPTER 20

Jason

I couldn't believe Jaz was actually talking to people. She asked everyone's name too. She asked a bunch of questions about what they liked to do, what kind of grades they got, and what their favorite subject was in school. I guess she did okay for someone with no social skills. I kind of thought it was because she liked the guy named Santiago on Team Touchdown.

The plane ride was fun, but I probably should have slept. My exhaustion hit me when we got off the plane. My legs felt shaky, and I was starving. When we got outside, the sun had come up and there were four limos parked in a row. They all had a sign on the front window, each with a different team name on it.

Before we got to our limo, the driver hopped out and opened the door for us. Steve filmed us grinning like two fools as we got in, then he climbed in with us. The limo had bottled water, soda, and a bunch of snacks, but I wanted real food. I grabbed a bottle of water while Jaz stuffed all of the snacks in the backpack.

"Why are you stealing the snacks?" I asked.

"I'm not stealing. They're ours. I don't want to have to spend money on food, just in case we need money for the next challenge."

I didn't say anything, but I was absolutely planning to buy food.

CHAPTER 21

Jazmine

Our limo drove us through the streets of
New York City and dropped us off in front of
a big, fancy hotel. When we checked in, the
clerk gave us one key, a gift card for the hotel
restaurant, and a *Treasure Hunt* envelope. I
was too tired for another clue, but I opened
it anyway. It was the best note yet because it
wasn't a clue after all: "Beginning at 10:00 a.m.,
you are on a mandatory three hour rest period.
You may not leave your room during this time."

Our hotel room was crazy. It was on the
twentieth floor, and it had a huge TV. I opened
the closet and found two robes inside.

"Jaz! Come here!" Jason was in the bathroom with the door open.

"Umm, no thanks."

"No," he said. "I mean, you have to see this."

There was a TV in the bathroom mirror. I touched it, but it was like it wasn't there. It was literally inside the mirror. You could do your hair and makeup and watch TV at the same time. The TV was on the hotel channel, so it only showed information about room service, the business center, and other things the hotel could help you with. Jason tried to change the channel, but the remote didn't work. He went to the TV in the bedroom. It would only show the hotel channel too.

Jason frowned. "Mandatory rest period means no TV?"

"No. I think TV means possible access to helpful information, so no TV."

"Oh."

Jason sat on the bed with the hotel menu. "Why are two eggs fourteen dollars?"

Everything on the menu was a rip off. We spent the whole gift card on breakfast. I was glad he decided to take a shower while he waited for his food. He really did stink—I wasn't just teasing him. Plus I needed some time alone. No Jason, no Steve, no camera.

We both fell asleep after we ate, but a knock at the door woke us up. I looked at the clock. The rest period was over. Jason peeked through the hole in the door. "It's Steve."

As soon as Jason let Steve in and shut the door, there was another knock. It was room service again. An older man wheeled in a tray with a silver covered dish on it. He took our breakfast cart with him when he left.

"We don't have time for you to eat again," I said. "Rest time is over."

Jason frowned. "But I didn't order anything else. Honestly."

Steve started filming as I pulled the lid off the dish. It was *Treasure Hunt: Clue Three*. This one was in a thick envelope. Before I could look inside, the pager buzzed. I grabbed it out of the backpack, and Jason looked over my shoulder. "Team Double Trouble Disqualified: Violation of rest period."

Big surprise, they cheated, I thought. *I knew there was something off about them.* "Figures. They were snobby anyway, with their Harvard-sweatshirt-wearing parents."

"Are you kidding?" asked Jason. "You're criticizing their Harvard sweatshirts? You're applying to Harvard. Anyway, they were nice. How can you assume they were trying to cheat?"

"I don't know, maybe they just thought the rules didn't apply to them." I rolled my eyes. "And were they nice when they laughed at you outside the hotel?"

Jason looked down. "They were nice on the plane."

"You know, that's your problem, Jason. You're too friendly. They were probably just being nice to make you lower your guard. They were stuck up."

He glared at me. "You're the one with the problem, Jaz! All you care about is yourself. You don't understand people because you have exactly one friend. And she's only nice to you because her mom *makes* her be nice." Jason clenched his teeth.

I couldn't believe he was embarrassing me like this on camera. "You can say what you want about me, but I'd rather have good grades than a bunch of friends. At least I'm not in a special reading class."

Apparently I went too far, because Jason did something I had never seen him do. He exploded. "SHUT UP. I *can* read. And I can certainly read people. I knew you had your own selfish reason for coming on this show. *I* wanted to buy a new home theater so we could all spend more time together as a family, but you want all the money for yourself. You're so foul, your own mama didn't want to send you on this show. She was worried you'd start some mess. I had to promise her I'd try to keep the peace. And I did try. But I'm done."

"What?" I couldn't believe it. *My own mother didn't trust me to act right on TV?*

"Yeah, Jaz. You think you know everything. You think you're so perfect. But my friendly personality has cracked every single clue so far. And you're so arrogant, I bet you thought it was all you."

"I didn't even know you *knew* the word arrogant." I knew that was going too far, but I didn't care.

Jason snatched the envelope out of my hand and sat on the bed. "From now on, we're doing this my way." He started reading a pamphlet.

We had already lost almost half an hour. "We have to go, Jason."

He glared at me until I looked away.

CHAPTER
22

Jason

I don't hate anyone, but if I did it would be Jazmine. It took *Treasure Hunt* for me to realize I didn't have to feel bad about myself. She'd never get anywhere with her personality.

I could feel her staring at me while I read the pamphlets in the envelope. I didn't care. I really was done. I was going to win this contest for Brian. Not only that, I was buying the home theater. There was no way my parents would let her keep all the money. I read the hotel brochure first. I took my sweet time too.

Jaz tried to grab the envelope from me. I stood up and used my size as a dare. She backed off and said, "It's been an hour. Everyone is probably running all over New York City right now."

I ignored her, pulling out a magazine about New York City. The cover was split into four sections. Each one showed a different place to visit: a ballpark, a train station, a city park, and a skyscraper. I read every single article.

Jaz sat on her bed, crossed her arms, and stared at me while I read one article after another. I liked being in control for once. The envelope included a thick guide about New York, but there was no way I could read that whole thing. We really would lose if I tried to do that. I looked at the table of contents so I would at least know what was in it. I found a clue inside. It was another riddle, but there was no way I was giving it to Jaz. I read it five times while she glared at me. *Good*, I thought. *She can see what it feels like to be ignored.*

People come from near and far,
By bus, by plane, by train, and car.
They do not mind the bustling crowd.

This one spot makes New York proud.
There are things to see, and eat, and drink;
Everything but the kitchen sink.
You can be up high or way down low,
You can take a tour whenever you go.
This is a place in movies and books;
A place with many crannies and nooks.

The last time I read it, I *knew* where we had to go. Jaz was right about one thing: the other teams were probably running all over New York City. But they didn't need to. This place was right underneath our hotel.

I put the papers in the envelope, threw it to Jaz, and said, "Let's go."

CHAPTER

23

Jazmine

I couldn't believe Jason. We sat in the hotel room for so long while he read that Steve turned his camera off. I was tempted to scream at Jason and snatch the clues away from him again, but I knew he would put up a fight like last time. While I waited for him to finish, I had way too much free time to think about what Jason said.

He was right about one thing. I didn't have friends. But he was wrong about why. By the time I got to high school, I realized the best chance for me to have the life I wanted when I grew up was to go to a good college.

I studied so hard I stopped hanging out with my friends. Then they stopped inviting me anywhere. I was alone all the time, so I studied more. Eventually, the only people who tried to talk to me were just trying to study with me because I was smart. I wasn't happy about it, but at least I would have the chance to start all over in college.

But Jason knew everyone in the entire school, and they all liked him. He could talk about me if he wanted to, but he didn't know the first thing about me. He didn't know what it was like being the little nerdy one. He didn't know what it was like spending all day surrounded by people you had to compete with. Jason is popular, and a popular kid would never understand what it's like to be me.

When Jason stood up and said, "Let's go," I was glad for the interruption.

He left the hotel room without looking back, with Steve following behind him. I had to jog down the hallway to keep up with them, and I tried to read the poem on the way. The paper jiggled and I couldn't read it until we got in the elevator. It made no sense to me at all. The treasure could be anywhere. The elevator doors opened right when I took out the magazine. I had just enough time to see there were four places featured on the cover. I had no idea which one Jason was taking me to.

"Jason, where are we going?"

"Let me worry about that."

I rolled my eyes. *Now he's the one being a jerk.*

But I *was* worried. Jason might have the clue totally wrong. "The poem said it was crowded. Are we going to the ballpark?"

Jason didn't answer.

"The park?" *Come on, Jason, tell me something*, I thought.

Jason walked faster through the hotel lobby. His eyes searched for something, but I didn't know what. He must have found what he was looking for because he made a sharp turn before we got to the hotel front doors. We ended up in some kind of maintenance hallway. I couldn't tell if it was part of the hotel.

"Where are we going?" I asked again.

Even though I was behind him, I could tell he was smiling. I wanted to wipe that smile right off his face. Finally I said, "If you don't answer me, I'm taking these clues and I'm going out on my own."

Jason just said, "Bye."

He called my bluff. We both knew the rules said we couldn't split up. We'd be disqualified. It would be so embarrassing if everyone got a message that said, "Team Williams Disqualified: Sibling rivalry." So I was stuck trailing behind my brother. It was the blind leading the blind.

There were glass doors at the end of the hall, and people rushed by. Jason pushed open a door and stopped. It looked like we were in an underground mall. There was a drug store, a place that sold fancy dresses, and a market. Jason turned left. We passed an electronics store and a place that sold watches. *This doesn't fit the clue at all*, I thought, panicking.

Jason rushed along like everyone else. People bumped into me, and I had to swerve to avoid them. Some of the people looked like they were coming from work. Some pulled suitcases on wheels. Some looked like they just had the worst day of their lives. I could totally relate to them. The whole time I was dodging people, I was on the lookout for Team Touchdown and Team Heartbeat. But for all I knew, they had already won.

Further along there was a big archway that said Main Concourse and opened into a large hall. Once we passed under that, I knew where we were. We were in a train station. There were smaller archways labeled with track numbers and a lighted sign with departure and arrival times.

Jason stopped to look at the sign.

"Are you sure this is where we're supposed to be?" I asked.

He glared at me. "Are you sure it isn't?"

"No," I mumbled. I wanted to go off on him about running into this plan without talking to me about it first, but now wasn't the time.

Jason seemed pretty confident this was the right place. I didn't get a chance to read any of the information, so all I could do was follow him. He looked to be stuck now, though. I tried not to stomp my foot in frustration. My eyes darted around the crowds, looking for anyone wearing a yellow or blue tracksuit.

"Give me the poem," he said.

I handed it to him and watched his lips move while he read it. "We need to check all the corners and not obvious places."

"We don't have time to check all the corners!" I screamed so loud my voice echoed. The people passing by moved away from me, which, honestly, was probably a good idea.

Jason

I could tell Jaz was furious. She didn't think I was right, but she couldn't tell me I was wrong because she had no idea where we were supposed to go. If we lost *Treasure Hunt*, this moment still made it all worth it. Especially since I was positive we were in the right place.

The article about the train station had a paragraph about all of the eateries and shops in the station. It actually said the line *find everything but the kitchen sink*, just like the poem. Not only that, but we were trying to *find* something—even if we didn't know exactly what it was. But I don't think it was the kitchen sink. Another paragraph said they had filmed movies here. Now I just had to figure out what to do next.

While I was trying to decide, Jaz shoved me hard. I stumbled into the room where the ticket machines were. Steve jumped out of the way, then aimed the camera at me.

"Why did you do that?" I demanded.

"Team Touchdown is here," she whispered frantically.

I tried not to panic. "Well, now we're stuck in a room with only one way out."

Jaz peeked out. "They're at the information desk. Maybe we can make a run for it."

"In our red outfits?" As soon as I said it, I knew what we needed to do. "Jaz, take off your jacket."

"What? Is that allowed?"

"We'll stand out in these. Just do it." I took off mine and threw it behind a ticket machine. Then Jaz did the same.

Team Touchdown was still at the information desk, talking to the person in the booth. I led Jaz and Steve up the nearest flight of stairs. When we got there we hid behind a sign until they left. I realized we were hiding outside of a restaurant, and the waitress was staring at us.

"Are you guys okay?" she asked.

"Yeah," I said. "But maybe you can help us?"

"I'll try."

I knew Jaz probably thought I was wasting our time again, but I didn't care. "We're trying to find hidden corners or secret places in the station. Nooks and crannies."

"Hmmm. The only thing I can think of is the Hall of Secrets," she said.

"What's that?" My heart thumped in my chest. I had a feeling that was *exactly* what I was looking for. I looked at Jaz, and instead of being frustrated, she looked as excited as I felt.

"It's an old spot in the station—it has the most beautiful architecture. And the design makes sound travel really well. They say if you stand in opposite corners and whisper into the wall, you can hear each other."

She gave us directions and we sprinted to the Hall of Secrets. It was on the far side of the station, and we were the only ones there. Jaz and I stood in separate corners like two boxers and faced the wall.

For a moment, I just stood there. Then I took a deep breath and asked, "Can you hear me?" I felt dumb talking to the wall.

"Oh! Yeah—I can!" Jaz's voice came back loud and clear.

If I had time I would have wanted to figure out how it worked, but with Team Touchdown wandering around somewhere, I knew we had to hurry. Before we could figure out what to do next, a woman walked into the hall.

"Does this really work?" she asked us.

I nodded. "It's weird."

"Will you whisper something to me?" Jaz gave me a "we don't have time for this" look, but I wasn't going to be rude.

I went back to my corner and whispered, "Hello."

"Helloooooooo," she said back. "I have something for you."

I turned around and she grinned. She walked over and handed me a key.

Our eyes widened in shock.

"What does it open?" I asked the woman.

She just smiled and disappeared up the stairs.

Jazmine

I stared at the key resting in Jason's palm in surprise. I didn't want to admit it, but Jason had this whole thing figured out just by sitting down and looking at the materials. He had been right this whole time. We didn't have to rush around. We needed to take some time to think. We needed other people's help.

"Now what?" I asked.

"I don't know. I guess we start trying doors."

We were like spies, sneaking around the train station, looking out for Team Touchdown and Team Heartbeat. We had to duck twice to avoid Team Touchdown, but we could tell they didn't have a key. We started by trying doors in the main hall, but the key didn't work on any of them. After a while, we were out of doors.

Jason stopped and looked around. "The tracks," he said.

I followed him through an archway that led to the tracks. Ramps led passengers down to where the trains stopped, but there weren't many people waiting in the middle of the afternoon. The trains ran below us, and a walkway ran the length of the building across them.

Jason found a door tucked behind a wall. "There are doors down here. It looks like there's a pattern. A door above each track."

"Jason, there are at least twenty tracks. That's going to take forever."

He turned to me and grinned. "Well then, we better run."

We ran from door to door trying the locks. After about five doors, I spotted Team Touchdown trying doors on the other end. I pointed them out, and Jason's eyes got big. For once, he didn't stand there and think about it.

Jason

There was only one thing to do, even though I hated it. I gave Jaz the key. She was faster than me when she ran, even though I had longer legs. She also had a steadier hand. She was our only hope. And if Team Touchdown got to the correct door first, we were out of luck. It was all a game of chance now, and the only advantage we had was speed.

I didn't have to tell Jaz what I wanted her to do. It was like in track, when they hand the baton to the last runner. I ran behind her as she tried door after door. A few people moved out of our way when they saw us coming.

We were definitely moving faster than Team Touchdown, even though they sped up when they saw us.

There were only five doors left between us and them. Jaz was so focused she didn't fumble at a single lock. Two doors down, the key worked.

Team Touchdown saw our door open and stopped running. They made their way to us with defeated looks on their faces. There was nothing for them to do now but watch.

Jaz pushed the door open just a tiny bit. I peeked in over her head. The room wasn't much bigger than a walk-in closet. There were cameras in the corners and screens on the wall. We could see ourselves and Team Touchdown behind us. Another screen showed Team Double Trouble sitting in their hotel room watching us on the TV. A third showed Team Red Ponytail back at the Lindale Chamber of Commerce building watching us. The last screen showed Team Heartbeat running up and down the bleachers at the ballpark. They never had a chance.

A man sat in a chair watching the screens. I said, "Excuse me?"

He didn't turn around. He just said, "Be right with you."

I tried to figure out why his voice was familiar. Then he turned around. Jaz and I cracked up. It was Mr. Beefy Burger himself. He grinned at us and said, "Fannnnn-taste-ic!"

He walked over and handed us each a bag of Mr. Beefy Burger food. "Congratulations! You must be hungry!"

"My little brother, Brian, loves your commercial!" I said, still laughing. "And your food. Can you say hello to him?"

Mr. Beefy Burger asked my brother's name, then faced the camera. "Helllllllloooooo, Brian! Thanks for your support. Mr. Beefy Burger is a proud sponsor of *Treasure Hunt*, and we're going to send you a Mr. Beefy Burger T-shirt!"

I looked at Jaz. She was already shoving fries into her mouth.

CHAPTER 27

Jazmine

Mr. Beefy Burger and Jason stood with me and we faced the camera. Mr. Beefy Burger said, "I have something for you!" He pulled something from his pocket.

When I saw another *Treasure Hunt* envelope I almost had a heart attack. We were supposed to be done. This was supposed to be where we got a gigantic fake check that said $20,000 on it. I was ready to go home. Mr. Beefy Burger handed the envelope to Jason, who looked like he wanted to cry. And not happy tears either.

Jason opened the envelope. Inside was a

normal-sized check for $20,000. I screamed and hugged Jason. I didn't think he would hug me back, but he did.

He turned to the camera and held up the check. "Bri! We did it! You're getting a new bike, man!"

I imagined Brian's face when he found out we won. He would be so happy. I wanted to say something on camera too.

I cleared my throat. "I have something to say. I owe Jason an apology. I said some really horrible things to him. He didn't deserve that. He is the kindest, most patient person I know. He's not dumb. He figured out the last clue totally by himself. I would have missed every clue in the packet, and we would have lost."

Jason looked at the ground, suddenly all shy. Steve aimed the camera at him, and he said, "Thanks, Jaz. I know you just wanted us to win."

I took Jason's hand and lifted it in the air. Team Touchdown and their cameraperson clapped for us.

Steve said, "Tell viewers what you'll do with the money."

Jason and I looked at each other. That was the twenty-thousand dollar question. Neither one of us wanted to answer it, either. As far as I was concerned, we'd done enough arguing on camera.

"Well?" said Steve.

At the same time, Jason and I said, "Split it."

ABOUT THE AUTHOR

Nikki Shannon Smith is from Oakland, California, but she now lives in the Central Valley with her husband and two children. She has worked in elementary education for over twenty-five years and writes everything from picture books to young adult novels. When she's not busy with family, work, or writing, she loves to visit the coast. The first thing she packs in her suitcase is always a book.

ESCAPE!
The ISLAND
THE ONE
The RIGHT NOTE
TREASURE HUNT
WARRIOR ZONE

MASON FALLS MYSTERIES

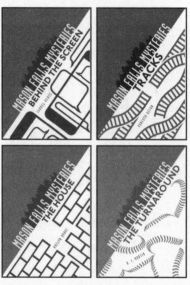

EVEN AN ORDINARY TOWN
HAS ITS SECRETS.

SUDDENLY
ROYAL

Becoming Prince Charming

Family Business

Next in Line

A Noble Cause

Royal Pain

Royal Treatment

**THE VALMONTS ARE NOT YOUR
TYPICAL ROYAL FAMILY.**